Copyright © 1997 by Nord-Süd Verlag AG, Gossau Zürich, Switzerland
First published in Switzerland under the title *Vom Glück ein dickes Schwein zu sein. . .*
English translation copyright © 1997 by North-South Books Inc.

First published in the United States, Great Britain, Canada,
Australia, and New Zealand in 1997 by North-South Books,
an imprint of Nord-Süd Verlag AG, Gossau Zürich, Switzerland.
Distributed in the United States by North-South Books Inc., New York.

Library of Congress Cataloging-in-Publication Data is available.
A CIP catalogue record for this book is available from The British Library.
ISBN 1-55858-706-3 (trade binding) 10 9 8 7 6 5 4 3 2 1
ISBN 1-55858-707-1 (library binding) 10 9 8 7 6 5 4 3 2 1
Printed in Belgium

For more information about our books, and the authors and artists
who create them, visit our web site: http://www.northsouth.com

Snail Started It!

Katja Reider • Angela von Roehl

TRANSLATED BY ROSEMARY LANNING

North-South Books • New York • London

One day Snail met a pig.
"My, you are fat!" said the snail. "I'm surprised your legs
   don't give way under all that weight!"
"I like being big and round," said Pig, admiring her
   reflection in a puddle.

"I'm just the right shape for rolling in the mud.
And besides, I enjoy my food!"

"I'm happy just the way I am." And with that,
Pig danced away on her dainty feet.

But when Pig thought about Snail's remarks,
she was upset. And so when she met a rabbit
hiding among the trees, she said to it,
"What a timid creature you are! Watch out,
or you'll worry your life away."

"Nonsense," muttered Rabbit. "I have to be careful, in case
the fox comes after me. I'm not going to let him catch me."
And with that he disappeared into a hole.

But Rabbit started thinking about what Pig had said.
He was so upset by it that later, when he met a dog
snoozing in the sunshine, he scolded him:
"What a lazy dog you are! All you ever do is sleep."
"Quite right," said Dog. "I have a good life, don't I?"

"I have wonderful dreams," he went on.
"Of cowardly cats, and juicy bones, and pretty poodles."
    And with that he closed his eyes and went back to sleep.

When Dog woke up, he remembered what Rabbit had said, and it upset him so much that he almost walked into a spider's web.

"Ugh!" said Dog, looking down his nose at the spider.
"What an ugly creature you are, with all those spindly legs."
"It can be useful to be ugly," Spider replied.
"People don't like the look of me, so they leave me alone."
And with that Spider scurried to the top of her web.

But the more she thought about the dog's unkind remark,
the more annoyed Spider became. When she saw a goose,
happily grazing in the meadow, she said:
"What a silly goose you are! How can you stay so calm when
  tomorrow you may be put in the cooking pot?"
"Tomorrow?" mused the goose. "Maybe. Maybe not.
Why worry about something I can't avoid?"

"I won't let such a gloomy thought spoil a lovely day,"
Goose declared, and she jumped into the cool, blue lake.

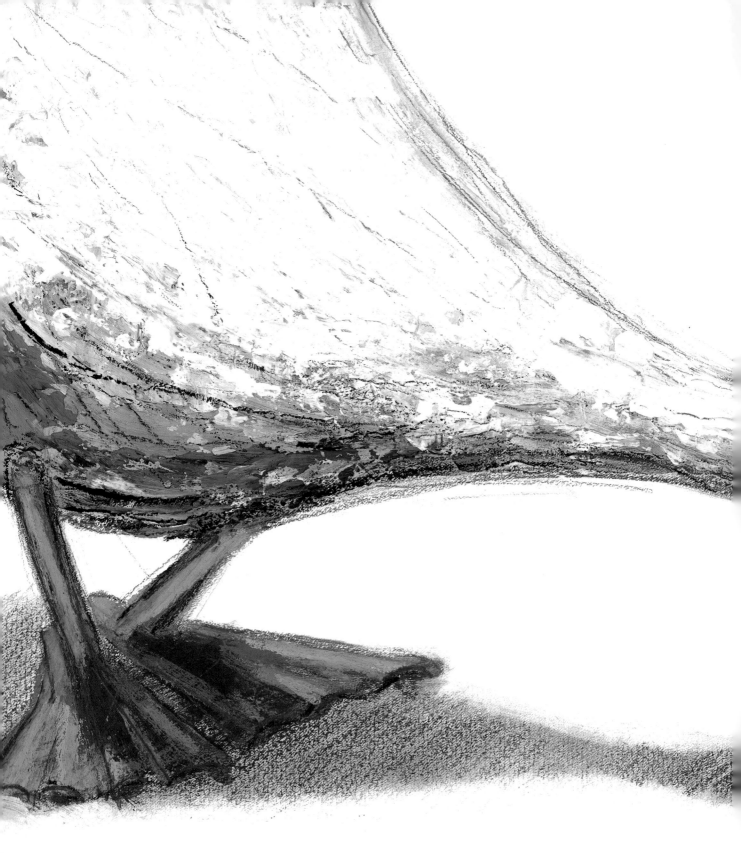

But Spider's words *had* spoiled the day for Goose,
and she was still upset when she met Snail.
"You are the slowest creature I've ever met!" she said.
"You were at the bottom of that same molehill when I
saw you this morning, and—"
"And now I've reached the top!" said Snail proudly.

"On my way up I've enjoyed the view, and I've had an interesting chat with the mole. It has been a good day."

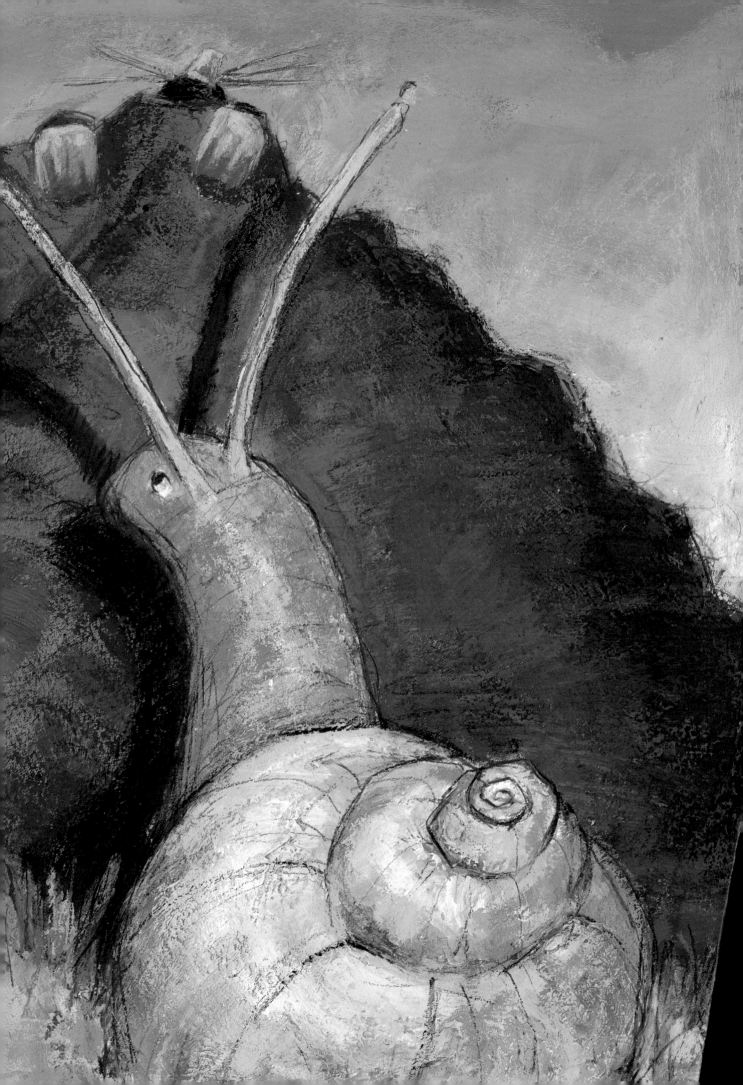

But it was not a good night for Snail, who sat in his shell and sulked.
"How dare she call me slow!" he said indignantly.
Suddenly he remembered what he had said to Pig.
Oh, no! he thought. I must go and apologize.

Early the next morning Snail set off to find Pig in her mud patch.
"I'm very, very sorry," panted Snail, quite out of breath.
"Sorry for what?" asked Pig.
"For calling you fat," said the snail. "I like you just as you are.
 A thin pig wouldn't look right at all."
"Why, thank you," said Pig.
 Then she remembered what she had said to Rabbit.
"You must excuse me, Snail. I have something important
 to do." And off she trotted to find Rabbit.

Before the day was out,
Pig had apologized to Rabbit,
Rabbit had apologized to Dog,
Dog had apologized to Spider,
Spider to Goose, and Goose to Snail.
And that night, with everything forgiven,
they all settled down to sleep contentedly,
happy once more just to be themselves.

DATE DUE

51-3 F			
9-23 IT			
9-30 IT			
2-23-2H			
3-8 IN			
4-26 2P			
3/10 46			